AF444187

QUARANCON PRESENTS

THROUGH SHADOWS

AN ANTHOLOGY OF AWARD-WINNING SPECULATIVE SHORT STORIES

EDITED BY PS LIVINGSTONE

A.M. JUSTICE · ALEX McGILVERY
J E HANNAFORD · LAURA SHANK
ANELA DEEN · LIAM HOGAN

Cover design by VM Designs
Stock art image by Grandfailure
QuaranCon dragon logo by Amy Gerardy
Interior formatting by VM Designs
Edited by PS Livingstone

Contents

FOREWORD
PS Livingstone

Winner 2020
Last Day at the Observatory
A.M. Justice
p. 1

First Runner-Up 2020
Old Superheroes Never Die
Alex McGilvery
p. 7

Second Runner-Up 2020
New Hope
J E Hannaford
p. 15

Second Runner-Up 2021
Wrangling Twisters
Laura Shank
p.25

First Runner-Up 2021
Job Security in an Apocalypse
Anela Deen
p.37

Winner 2021
Re-Boot
Liam Hogan
p.45

FOREWORD

FOUR WORDS. DEDICATION. Generosity. Inclusion. Community.

The life of a writer isn't an easy one. For many of us, it's not a choice – it's an urge, a need deep inside that compels us to tell stories. Publishing is even harder, whether indie or traditional. Gatekeepers, naysayers, finances, your own chronic self-doubt, all stand in the way of realising that dream: to see the culmination of your imagination in print. Then, in 2020, the pandemic hit.

What I say now, I say for myself, although I know many of you share these feelings. I lost family to COVID, lost my creativity, lost so many of my connections to the world. And then I found something … QuaranCon, Virginia McClain's brainchild, rose to fill the void. From the miasma came a tweet, a simple message asking if anyone would like to be involved in an online SFF convention. She didn't want money or gratification. She wanted to create something, an event where everyone was welcome and everyone could contribute. I hopped on the train.

In those early days, I had no idea what QuaranCon would become, no idea if we'd pull it off or anyone would turn up. But the response was overwhelming. Writers, editors, artists, bloggers and fans from across the globe offered their time and expertise, and five awesome days of original content streamed live. All for free.

We hoped QuaranCon wouldn't be needed again, that the pandemic would be resigned to the past. Of course, that didn't happen. In 2021, lockdown continued, so QuaranCon came back stronger. More content and more artists, building a diverse, welcoming community event. We're proud of what we've achieved and unbelievably grateful for the kindness and friendship of everyone who made it a reality.

In both 2020 and 2021, we ran short story competitions, a chance for writers to show a snapshot of their incredible talent. As ever, we were bowled over by the response but even more so by the quality, making choosing a winner tough for our judges. This anthology, *Through Shadows*, is a collection of the top three stories in each year.

After so much sacrifice and hardship, we're still finding our way through COVID and whatever the world will be when it's over. *Through Shadows* is a testament to our short fiction themes of isolation and invention, as well as the ingenuity and dedication of a small group of people with open minds and kind hearts.

PS Livingstone

WINNER
2020

Last Day at the Observatory
A.M. Justice

TWENTY MINUTES LEFT to live. The icy wind cuts deep, but not as deep as the Shadow. Shadow of death – mine, everyone's. When it was farther off, six hours away at the edge of the horizon, it reminded me of the shadow the Earth casts on its own atmosphere at dusk, a grey wash arcing above the edge of all things. Now it's as black as pitch, a wall stretching from sea to sky, north to south, limitless and inexorable, blotting out the stars.

Inside, my back presses against the door. Warm air blows down from the ceiling vents but can't push the cold from my blood. I've spent my life studying celestial anomalies and in twenty minutes one is going to kill me. My heart is a trapped wren, flitting and flapping, held prisoner by ribs, stuck in the clutches of lungs that insist on doing their job. I'm still breathing, even if my ears hear those breaths as sobs. I came to the top of this mountain to see the beginning of time, not the end.

The Shadow is behind this door. It's coming, fifteen minutes away. Knees weak, chest tight, I slide to the floor, creep into the control room, anxious for a place to hide. Sam's red high tops sprawl out from behind the second monitor. On one shoe, the shoelaces hang loose, snarled in a knot, aglets dangling. Sloppy dresser, Sam. Not a sloppy death, though: asphyxiation with a plastic bag. That was tidy. Leave it to Sam to MacGyver his way out of this.

The second monitor beeps with fresh data, like it's been doing every thirty seconds since we lost Tonga eighteen hours ago. Almost eighteen hours. It must be aliens, we said in emails and phone calls that spider-webbed from observatories and military bases all over the world. It started at midnight on New Year's Day at the International Dateline, for God's sakes. The Australians, the Japanese, the Chinese, and Russians sent probes and then teams into the dark. They learned nothing, equipment and men swallowed by the void. There was that Aussie reporter who tried to stay ahead of the leading edge. Poor dumb woman didn't realise how fast the world turns, but what a panic after her live feed blipped out. Riots in Hong Kong and Shanghai, Mumbai on fire, the crush of bodies seeking a last blessing in Mecca. Back on the Mainland people were loading up their semiautomatics, some barricading themselves behind steel doors, others squealing through town in pickups, howling and shooting. More riots in New York and Atlanta, Chicago, Houston. Everyone without a gun rubbing shoulders with neighbours packed into every last church and temple and mosque in America. I wish I'd gotten through to Mom but never heard anything but that damn woman telling me the lines were busy and to try again later. An hour before sunset, the phone lady went silent. God, last time I talked to Mom was two months ago. I'd meant to call on Christmas. Damn the time difference.

Three minutes to midnight. My last three minutes hiding under my desk, whimpering. I could go outside and face the void. That would be heroic. My cheeks dry, my breath quiet, I'm shivering. It's cold up on this mountain, but not inside. Power's still on. I think the wren caged in my chest has hoarded all the blood for herself. Shit, the damn thing beeped again. Two and a half minutes. How's that song go? "Daisy, daisy, dah dah dah dah da dum." Crap, I could never remember that stupid song. What if Sam had stuck it out? Would I have— God no, last man on Earth— yuck, no. I hate being alone, though. I wish I'd gotten through to Mom.

There's another beep. Down to one minute. If I'm wrong about God? Well, if I end up in Hell, at least I'll get to find out what the heck this thing is that's going to kill me. A little snort flares my nostrils, and my lips curl up. Ears prick as the last beep sounds, and silence cuts it off.

FIRST
RUNNER-UP
2020

OLD SUPERHEROES NEVER DIE
ALEX MCGILVERY

"SUPERMAN HAS CLARK Kent when he wants to kick back and just not go out to fight the bad guys. I've worn this costume for so long I can't remember what name my mother called me. It gets tiring sometimes. There are days I could use an extra hand, but who offers to carry groceries for a guy in a superhero costume? Even if the guy qualifies for his old age security." The old man sat in the chair in my office and glowered at me. The blue spandex might have been a good choice when he was younger and in better shape, but now it showed off the softness of his old body. Not that he was soft. That gun was real enough, and his eyes held the same steel as the gun.

"What do you want me to do?" I asked and looked at the blank page where I would normally have reams of notes.

"I need a retirement home," the old man said. "Someplace where the bad guys can't find me, and where everyone else will leave me alone."

"I need a name, a social security number, an address," I said. "I understand you wanting a rest, but I can't place a nameless stranger in a home. You have to give me something."

He pushed himself to his feet. The sound of joints popping and cracking made me wince. His fingers were swollen. Super-arthritis? Was surgery even possible on him?

"Come with me," he said. "See for yourself. Don't get too close and don't get in my way."

I followed him out of my office and watched him walk along the street. Nobody paid the slightest attention to him. A flock of pigeons flew over him and left their mark on his blue costume. His shoulders sagged a little as he kept walking, though I noticed his hand brush against that gun at his side. I don't know if he walked slowly so I could keep up, but if so, he overdid it. Several times I had to stop to tie my shoe or look in a window to give him the space he needed.

We turned down a ramp into a parking garage. Shouts echoed through the empty space as men in black ninja costumes jumped out to surround him. None of them saw me as I ducked between two cars and pulled out my cell phone. No signal.

My debate as to whether I should go out on the street to call for help ended when the ninjas leaped to the attack. In the movies, they'd charge one by one and allow him to defeat one before the next moved in. This wasn't the movies. They struck as a coordinated team to pummel the old man.

Only he didn't move like an old man now. One opponent advanced a little too fast. The man in spandex grabbed him by the throat and tossed him at those attacking from the rear. The smack of a fist hitting flesh reached my hiding place, a momentary strike before the hero used the assaulter's arm to pull the ninja off balance and shove him down with a quick jab. He spun out of an attempted headlock by another opponent and threw that man on top of the first, hard enough to make him bounce.

One by one, the ninjas joined the pile of unconscious thugs until it was taller than the old man. The last one he dispatched with a jump kick I couldn't imagine trying, though I was sure he had thirty years on me. As I came out of my hiding place, the energy left him and he puffed like I did if I walked up a hill too fast. He waved at me, and I waited for him to catch his breath.

"Why didn't you use that?" I pointed at the gun at his side.

"Do you know ... how much ... ammunition costs?" he said between wheezes. "Nobody pays me for this." He walked to the back of the garage and pulled the cover off a classic muscle car. Well, it would have been a classic if it weren't for the fifty calibre machine guns mounted on each door.

"You may as well get in." He waved me over to the passenger side and climbed into his seat.

"Where are the seatbelts?"

"Never needed them." He pushed a button and the engine roared to life. Smoke filled the garage as tyres squealed; then he released the brake and we took off. He careened through the garage, slowing only slightly to bump a reviving ninja back onto the pile with a rear fender. We erupted out of the lot and onto the street, where he had to slam on the brakes to fit into the bumper-to-bumper traffic.

"Walking would be faster," I said.

"Tell me about it." The old man thumped the steering wheel and glared up at the flock of pigeons that left white gooey marks across the windshield. "Flying's better, but everyone's so uptight now I'm afraid they'd try to shoot me down. Got some nice pictures the first time they scrambled on me, but now it's just a nuisance."

He pulled off the road and sped away through an alley, making one turn after another into spaces in which I was sure we'd never fit. Even with the extra width of the guns, we didn't leave a scratch on the walls.

"Here we are," he said, whipping the car through an open loading door. The car rocked and creaked as the elevator lifted us up to the top floor.

We stopped and he climbed out of the car. I had to climb across the driver's seat to get out.

"Don't hit any buttons," he said.

The words rocket launcher peeked out from beneath my hand. I moved it away and made sure to watch what I did until I stood safely outside the car.

The penthouse was sparsely furnished, almost barren. I shivered. It might be a great hero's lair, but I wouldn't want to live there.

"Tea, coffee?" the old man said. "I'd offer you biscuits and jam, but jam jars are my one weakness."

"How can a jam jar be your weakness?"

"Can't open them," he said, "never could." He poured boiling water into a pot and swirled it, then made tea.

"Was a time I didn't mind it up here," he said. "I needed a quiet place to get away from the rush; being a superhero is addictive. Then, like any addiction, it takes over and you lose yourself. Those guys with their secret identities had it right. You've got to step back and let it go once in a while."

"So why not take off the mask and retire?" I watched him stir the tea in the window's reflection.

"I'm not sure who's under there anymore." He came over and handed me a cup. I sipped at it. I hate tea, but its bitterness seemed appropriate. He stared through the window at the city. From up here, it looked quiet and peaceful.

"They'd find you anywhere I might place you," I said. "Unless you take off the mask and become just another old man."

He drank his tea slowly and I waited. When I finished my tea, I left him there, still looking out of the window. I saw him wave once before I closed the door behind me.

SECOND
RUNNER-UP
2020

New Hope
J E Hannaford

I HATED WINDS. The chill permeated our cave, and the community shivered in perpetual cold. This year's short Winds had taken a heavy toll; our sericlave had grown too swollen on previous years of plentiful food.

Numbers of dead increased daily, adults and children alike. Deaths from starvation, from cold and accidents in the pit through sheer exhaustion. The bellows worked hard and fast to keep those who lived at the top of the peak warm and happy. My own muscles ached from the daily grind of shovelling ash.

I missed my family more than ever. Ussid had died at the start of the season, and I had been alone ever since. She'd been my companion since my Leaving, had taken me into her home and made it my own. It was lonely enough being Untouched, let alone living alone too. Occasional snatched visits with my brother weren't enough anymore, and although I hadn't been in touching distance of her for years, I missed seeing my mother around the cave. She died in the middle of the season.

I was utterly broken and alone.

Then I took in my first and only hut mate. We'd never have another while we both lived in Dragonsbreath. I must have been about 25 cycles – it's hard to count age when you live underground. That young girl changed my life. She gave me something to live for.

~

I remember the day I first saw her, all skin and bones, maybe ten cycles old and straggling after her big brother like a lost infant. Burn it, but I empathised with her.

We sat at the back of the council chamber, me and a few of the others, the reed-woven walls bulging with the sheer number of the sericlave squeezed in. Even us, the Untouched, were allowed access for the last meeting of the season.

Rains was due, the clouds building on the horizon, and finally it was time to start our year anew.

The usual statements opened the meeting: disciplines for falling asleep on the job, how many deaths this tide – too many – how much food we didn't have left. All I wanted to know was when I'd feel the sun on my skin, be drenched in life-giving rain and feel plants beneath my feet.

Once that was done, a woman stood up, pushing her son forward.

He looked reluctant, but as she jabbed him repeatedly in the back, he shuffled towards the elders, and that skeletal young girl trailed behind.

"I speak for my hut," he mumbled.

My father rose, imposing even when half-starved. Before the boy had even spoken, he had spotted the girl, and his eyes sought mine. He raised an eyebrow in question, and I nodded.

To this day, I wonder if he knew what he was doing. If he knew how low I truly was.

"Speak."

The boy grasped his sister by the arm and bent down to whisper to her, then he gave her a hug. A rare sight from anyone to an Untouched. Trembling and tearful, she stepped alongside him, a little more strength in her spine than before.

"My sister needs a new home."

We all knew what those words really meant. She was too old to stay in the community, had started to bleed; it was too risky for her to get involved with a boy. Burn it, but she was so young.

I had been older, and the tender care Ussid had shown me in those first few months was life-changing. Empathy had poured from her, seasoned with kindness and love. I didn't know if I could do the same. After all, Ussid had taken many girls under her wing. This child would be my first.

"Will anyone here take this child into their home?" The traditional words. Never a reason, never an explanation, you never knew when an Awldrin would appear.

She was tiny, and it was now my job to raise this child to be a strong woman, a survivor.

I stood. "I have space in my hut." The girl's eyes widened, maybe she had expected someone older. I quickly added, "And my heart," then smiled at her. Watcher knew I was trying to reassure her, to make her feel welcome.

My father smiled. "Thank you, Laytha. You may both leave now. Is there any other business?"

"Aye, I speak for my hut," a man called from the benches.

I wove through the seating, their mother's tear-streaked face following my every move. The two children had moved to the door of the hut.

I met them there.

"Thank you for being brave and bringing your sister to her Leaving," I said to the boy.

"Will I be able to see her again?" he asked.

"We will find a way, I promise." It was the first of many promises I made Makin, and I have kept them all.

"Will she be okay?"

"She will be more than okay. She will be loved and fed, she will learn all I can teach her, and she will always know you love her. Which is your hut?"

The boy pointed at a hut on the opposite side of the cave to my own.

"Is her bag ready?"

"I can speak for myself," she interrupted, and at that moment I knew she would be just fine. She flung her arms around her brother.

"I'll see you soon. Make sure Ma eats, work hard, and don't worry about me. We always knew today would come. It's just sooner than we hoped. Laytha, which is my new home?"

My heart lightened a little as her positivity outshone the wretchedness of her body.

"That one," I said, pointing.

"It's directly across from yours. Makin, I'll wave to you when the crystal turns green each day."

"Why green?" he asked.

"Because, green is hope, green is plants and food in Rains."

"Green is my shift," I murmured.

"Then you will be my new hope."

"And I'll put my hope in you too," Makin added.

~

We settled into a routine quickly after that. I taught her to weave and cook until Rains came. Every day we filed out of the cave to work in the fields, revelling in the warm sun on our backs. Here, I taught her to nurture the plants, never to let even the smallest shoots give up because we needed them in the future as much as they needed us now. It was a life lesson I had no idea she would take so personally.

We'd watch the younger men racing up and down the glassy slopes, carrying news and crops back to the Elders.

One day, she squealed with joy as her brother made his first run.

"Laytha, he made it! He did it!" She jumped up and down with effusive joy. "Do you think I could do the run?"

"You could … but you can't."

"What about when no one is watching?"

I pointed at her feet. "You don't have stickies. With them, you might be able to." I grinned at her as an idea began to bloom. She had brought joy back to me and I wanted to return the favour.

Later that night, I snuck out of our home and sidled around the cave to my brother's hut. Years ago, we had agreed on a series of signals. He still set them every night, allowing me to know when he was alone. His shoes were outside the right-hand side of the door. It was safe to see him.

A whispered conversation later, and I returned with a gift hidden under my clothes. For the first time in years, excitement kept me awake all night.

I heard her rise and left my nook to join her for breakfast. She had already started preparing it when I joined her, holding the treasure behind my back.

"What have you got, Laytha? Why are you grinning?" Her excitement rose as I laughed, backing away from her. She jumped up and ran toward me.

"What is it? Tell me!"

I brought out a small pair of old stickies, and she whooped with joy.

"Are they for me? Can I try them? Oh, Laytha, thank you."

And so it began.

Every night after work, my brother hung back looking authoritative, sending people back to the cave. It wasn't something he found hard. He was being groomed to take our father's position. Then we'd pop out of our hiding place and he'd run ahead of us. She would chase, following each footstep up the glassy slope, reaching the top flushed and elated, practising all through Rains and well into the burning heat of Canicule. She treasured those footwraps, and I found I treasured her.

Nothing was too challenging, no slope too steep, no section too jagged. She fell and lacerated her legs more times than I could count that first cycle. Each time I patched her up, and she'd go again.

Then Winds returned. That year, it was long, and we both lost our remaining parent. We clung to each other for comfort and support. Without her, I would simply have faded away.

To this day, I don't think she knows. To her, I am her safe place, a comforting figure. She has no idea how she saved me that day in the Elders' hut.

And now … now, I have to let her go, for by the Watcher's mighty wings, she may save us all.

SECOND
RUNNER-UP
2021

Wrangling Twisters
Laura Shank

TENISH STARED AT the angry, churning clouds above, crackling with strips of fuchsia light. Torrents of rain pounded the ground. Crouched under the cover of the trees, he waited with Alleita. Fields sprawled before them, washed out by the unnatural green hue of the sky.

"Just a thunderstorm," Alleita asked. "Or more?"

"Not sure," Tenish said, buzzing with anticipation.

More Wranglers and Protectors rushed to join them, a crowd growing as the storm built. Then the hail came.

Tenish let out a whoop, bursting from the safety of the trees. Alleita grabbed him by the tunic, pulling him back.

"Wait a moment," she said. She unclipped her shield, holding it over her head, motioning for Tenish to do the same.

He sighed but unclipped his as well.

"Always a Protector," he teased.

Alleita rolled her eyes but smiled.

"How are you going to Wrangle with a concussion?" She nodded at the thick chunks of ice striking the ground.

He grinned. She was right, as usual.

They sprinted into the storm, hail bouncing off the shields they held aloft. Tenish whooped again as a spout formed in the clouds.

"I knew it!" he shouted over the wind and hail.

Alleita stuck close to his side. "Did you forget something?" she shouted back.

Tenish frowned, looking down. His gloves!

She reached into her pouch and handed them to him. "What would you do without me?" she said.

"Catch magic with my bare hands."

"Powerful, but not practical."

"Perhaps." Tenish shrugged. "I've always wondered what it would feel like." Alleita frowned and Tenish sighed. She was always so serious. "It was a joke," he said. He had wondered, though.

Tenish pulled on his gloves while Alleita directed the Wranglers and Protectors. In minutes, they had fallen into formation. Years of training and drills made Twisters routine, even if there was nothing routine about them.

The group split into a wide circle around the field, twenty feet apart with the aim of having the Twister's touchdown point in the centre.

The hail thinned. Tenish lowered his shield, squinting at the clouds. The storm seemed to be abating. He knew better, though. Everyone learned to spot Twisters at a young age. Tenish flexed his gloved hands.

The wind fell; his ears rang in the quiet.

"It's time," Alleita said, sword drawn.

Tenish nodded. He glanced across the field, fifteen Wranglers spaced throughout, their Protectors behind them. The arrival of a Twister could spawn a battle, villages fighting for the resources hidden inside, though it had been years since it'd happened. Still, he liked knowing Alleita was at his back.

The Twister churned in the sky. Tenish stood, awed. Even with all his time as a Wrangler, the thick clouds, how they twisted in an unnatural and awesome way, still amazed him.

"There!" Tenish pointed. The rotating winds reached toward the earth, and the Wranglers adjusted their line, preparing for touchdown. Tenish's heart thudded, adrenaline surging. The spout landed with a thundering roar in the middle of their wide circle, blinding him with dirt and grass. Even so, Tenish caught glimpses of magenta swirls hidden within the raging wind.

Bracing himself, he walked steadily toward the storm cloud. Tenish wriggled his fingers, itching to get started. He knew Alleita followed behind him, close enough to protect but far enough to avoid getting sucked into the winds.

Nothing could protect him from that.

Wranglers danced a thin line between life and death, between glory and defeat. For the village to survive, for him to survive, he needed to disable the Twister as fast as possible.

Tenish reached up, only feet from the wall of air. Wisps of it slipped through his hands as he grabbed for the twinkling fuchsia light disguised in the cloud of wind. He pulled out a strand, the buzzing of it steadied by his gloves, although he sensed the raw power contained within.

Gritting his teeth, Tenish stepped backwards, one foot at a time. This was the hard part. He slowly unravelled the magic. It shone brightly, blinding in the dim light.

Head down, he exited the debris cloud. Beyond, it was easier to run back to the Collectors. He handed the magic off, the Collector taking it in her thick gloves, much sturdier than his thin, flexible ones. Tenish could snatch magic from the wind, but Collectors crushed it into cauldrons, infusing the water inside with its power. One Twister filled dozens of cauldrons.

Tenish turned back. Two more strands had been pulled from either side of the Twister, his fellow Wranglers on their way to hand them off. Alleita scanned the horizon, ever the watchdog.

He passed close to her on his way back, and she broke her focus long enough to perform their trademark triumphant handshake.

"Betcha can't get two more before it's gone," she teased. Tenish put on a face of mock outrage as he ran back.

Two strands before the Twister extinguished? She'd thrown him a challenge. The spout dodged and weaved, creeping across the field; never predictable, never in an exact path. Tenish sprinted closer with his arms stretched into the sky, instinct and training kicking in as he grabbed one of the magenta strands that whipped through the air.

The Twister sucked the Wrangler next to him off his feet, as if to prove its power. The man flew into the air, his mouth open in a scream Tenish couldn't hear. Tenish cursed, stumbling back, but kept hold of the strand in his hand, heaving with all his might. The magic pulled back, threatening to sweep him away as well. Step by step, Tenish dragged himself far enough to get to the Collector.

He wiped his forehead. Though the Twister still raged, it had shrunk. They were getting close. Pushing through his fatigue, he ran to it, this strand separating much easier than the first two.

Tenish almost released it when he saw men rushing from the forest.

Twisters came once every few years – if you were lucky. Tenish had seen its magic cure a merchant's lame leg after a spill off his horse. Last year, the village had used their precious supply to replenish the crops when beetles ate three quarters of the plants. And they used magic to strengthen their protections, especially around the magic itself.

He clung to his strand, staring. There were rules about this, about who the magic belonged to, but desperate men ignored them. Usually, the Protectors could hold them off, but as more fighters poured from the forest, Tenish's heart sank. This was no village squabble. This was an army of men pounding toward them, weapons above their heads, yelling screams of battle he couldn't hear over the rushing wind.

There's too many of them!

The Wranglers and Protectors had been split across the field. A group stood with Tenish, behind the Twister as it cut toward the forest. The others were scattered across from them. Directly in the path of the army.

The attackers fell upon the Protectors and Wranglers in a blur of steel and blade. Alleita rushed ahead of Tenish, bellowing a war cry and falling into battle stance, forming a line with the nearby Protectors in front of him and their Wranglers.

No! Tenish glanced around wildly. *I have to do something!*

He took a deep breath. *Focus.*

He wanted to pick up a sword and stand with Alleita, to fight instead of retreat, but he forced himself to rip his eyes from her. He had to do his job; she had to do hers. His training dictated that he needed to finish with this strand. He could do that.

But he hated retreating while his people, his friends, fought to protect him.

Get to the Collector.

He ran toward her, pulling the strand. She reached for it, but a spear pierced her side. Blood gushed from the wound and she screamed, falling from the wagon. The attacking men had split, coming for the infused cauldrons.

The Wrangler next to Tenish took a knife to the arm and lost her grip on the strand she carried. The magic snapped back into the Twister. Tenish cursed, pulling against the added weight. Wranglers and Protectors and army alike flew into the air, as the direction of their fighting led them too close to the Twister's path.

Tenish's blood pounded in his ears. His mind raced. He needed to do something. Alleita matched two men blow for blow as they fought. A scream split the air and the Protector beside her fell. Tenish stood only twenty feet behind, still holding his strand of magic. Alleita took a blow to the side, her armour cracking. She stumbled, but stayed standing. Another blow knocked off her helm, exposing her head.

We're going to lose.

Tenish had trained his whole life as a Wrangler. There were rules. There was protocol. There were gloves. But if he didn't do something, right now, Alleita would die. And most likely, so would he.

The Twister screamed, turning toward them in a zig-zag, scattering men and Protectors alike. Alleita stumbled back, her brow dripping blood.

Through it all, he held onto the magic.

Gripping it with all his strength, Tenish transferred it to one hand. His muscles strained as he stripped off the glove on his other hand with his teeth.

"Tenish!" Alleita screamed, cutting down a soldier that rushed toward him. She watched him with crazed eyes. "You don't know how to wield it! What are you doing?"

Always a Protector.

"Catching magic!" he shouted back, then reached out with his bare hand.

He gripped the strand of crackling fuchsia light, letting out an involuntary scream as it exploded inside him. It burned, as if he had stepped into a fire.

I'm going to die. Pain ripped through his body. *What was I thinking?*

But still, he held on, not letting go, not letting it overtake him.

The pain subsided as suddenly as it had come. Somehow, he felt the magic concede. His eyes shot open.

Pink tinted his vision. Power crackled in his fingers. Alleita gaped at him. Tenish laughed and turned toward the soldiers.

FIRST
RUNNER-UP
2021

Job Security in an Apocalypse
Anela Deen

THE END OF the world came on a Monday afternoon.

It was pretty exciting, if I'm honest. I'd fallen into a rut with my daily routine, finishing tasks by rote, and more often than not, contemplating whether there was any point to suffering through constant doldrums for so little reward. No one ever appreciated how hard I worked. No one ever smiled when I showed up. It got to you after a while.

So, when the world came crashing down, I didn't mind at first. Talk about a shake-up. Fire and broken glass. A smoke-riddled sky and burning rains. Fear as thick as smog and pavements shiny with blood. Granted, such things weren't entirely novel, but the scale of it certainly was. Boredom became a distant memory during that initial stretch of days, racing from one place to another, trying to stay ahead of it. And yeah, we can talk about how the fall of mankind wasn't unexpected with the way things carried on between people and nations, but nothing prepares you for the reality of it actually happening.

Just as nothing prepares you for what comes after the fires burn out and the bad rains stop. The stories don't talk about the situation later, once roving bands of thieves and barbarian kings have sacked the sanctuaries kinder survivors managed to create. They don't say what happens once apocalyptic scarcity sets in, and need plays out its self-destructive game until the final sparks sputter and die.

And now they never will, so I'll just tell you.

It gets really quiet. Not the quiet of night-time, like the normal world knew it. I'm talking the total absence of human voices, here. Not a hush, but a void.

I wandered through that scarred landscape and reflected on everything I'd taken for granted. I asked myself: Had it really been so bad? Life was meant to be annoying. Agitation keeps the molecules spinning. It's the engine of innovation. Look, I never could stand people, but without them, when it was only me and that awful silence, I realised my mistake. If one's existence depended on the world functioning merrily along, an apocalypse was really inconvenient. Without purpose, there's only oblivion.

In case you're wondering, yes, I was starting to feel sorry for myself.

It was about then I came across that group of kids.

There was a lot of screaming when they saw me.

So much screaming.

My skull rang for a good five minutes after the oldest one – a plucky, twelve-year-old girl – managed to quiet them down. Why are small people so loud? I went ahead and asked her this.

She propped dirty fists to the waist of her threadbare dress, her little face smeared with dirt and wreathed in chaotic curls, and said, "They're scared of strangers."

I bet they were. I bet they'd never seen anything so terrifying as the desperation of adults. How they'd survived on their own for so long was a mystery.

"There aren't any strangers out here anymore," I told her.

"You're a stranger."

"Not really. I'm sure you've seen me around."

She didn't like that answer. She got pretty angry, in fact. Pointed a finger at me. "This is all your fault," she accused. "You're the reason this happened."

I've gotta to tell you, I took that personally. I mean, really. The world ends and I still get blamed for everyone's problems? As if they weren't and haven't always been responsible for their own miseries? I put this fact to her exactly so.

Her eyes went a little misty then, that firm lower lip wobbling despite her tenacious glare. She swiped at her face with scraped up palms, and I felt very much like the bastard folks used to call me.

"What should we do if everyone's gone?" she asked, her question chorused by meeker whimpers from the gaggle of little ones she'd been shepherding. "Should we give up?"

Let me explain something about clarity. It hits like a lightning bolt. There I stood, in the ruin of the world I'd felt ill-appreciated me, and realised how little I'd appreciated the world. You didn't have to love every aspect of something to mourn its loss, and you didn't have to be the most well-equipped soul to take a step toward a different path. The old saying was wrong, you know. Opportunity didn't announce itself with a knock. It came in whispers and nudges, and only for those who paid attention.

I was paying attention.

So, I told her, "No, you're not giving up."

"Why not?" she asked, but I could tell she wasn't arguing. She wanted a reason she could believe in.

"If all of you survived, others must have as well. We're going to find them, and then we're going to head somewhere better. Somewhere green."

She lifted a brow, her curious gaze touching on my dark cloak's fraying hem and the curve of the scythe I carried with me.

"We?" she asked.

"Sure, why not?"

"Helping people to live isn't your normal line of work."

"I don't mind expanding my résumé."

She considered the idea, though it was obvious she still didn't trust me entirely. That was okay. She was right to be afraid.

"Think of it as job security for me," I said. "There's no point to my existence without yours."

"That's true," she allowed.

"So, what do you say? Should we give it a try?"

She smiled at me then. Me. The one nobody ever greeted with anything but dread. Reaching out, she took hold of my skeletal fingers and gave them a shake.

"Let's do it."

And that's how it went. My purpose these days? Collect the seeds of the old world and give them safe passage to better soil so they might one day bloom again. I'm enjoying the change of pace, if you want the truth. After all, there can be no winter without spring. No wheat to harvest without first planting grain.

Is it ironic that I'm a part of the beginning of the story rather than the end? Absolutely. Life is never more ridiculous – or more interesting – than when it's reinventing itself.

Take it from someone who used to only sit on the sidelines.

WINNER
2021

RE-BOOT
LIAM HOGAN

THE END OF the world began on Thursday the 8th of October 2026. A simple mutation in the virus that Singularity AIs used to lay down their bio-pathways. With frightening efficiency, it attacked all brain cells, genetically modified or not. By Friday afternoon, half-a-dozen bunker-dwelling survivalists were all that remained of the human race.

Of them, only I was properly prepared for the end of the world.

Only I had built a time machine.

I built it expressly for this purpose, for this Armageddon scenario. It was far too dangerous to use except when all was lost. But, when all was lost, it was our last – our only – hope.

I went back to 2021 to fix it. A change to the chemistry the pioneering bio-engineers had used, just before the Singularity rendered any further human innovation redundant. A change that meant the virus would never make the fateful and fatal leap from the lab to the rest of the world.

When I returned, the bunker's automatic lights flickered on and an air of abandonment greeted me. Which was as I'd expected, as I'd hoped it would be; my shelter made unnecessary by my heroic actions. Eagerly, I checked the data feed to confirm my manipulation had been successful.

The world had ended on the 25th of September 2022.

The final upgrade to the Large Hadron Collider at CERN breached some arcane physical constraint between this universe and the next. The resultant storm of dark-matter annihilations had torn away the Earth's protective atmosphere.

I ventured five years earlier and released a hungry beech marten into the LHC workings. Regrettably, the resultant outage would mean that the full potential of the collider would never be realised, but at least the Earth would be safe.

Back in my bunker, I once again checked the feeds.

The world had ended on the 23rd of February 2020. A communications error during the heat of post-Brexit talks, nerves rattled by the outbreak of the coronavirus, then only just being seen for the worldwide pandemic it would become. The UK unleashed its ageing Trident nuclear deterrent on the major European capitals, Brussels first and foremost. Triggering an instantaneous Dr Strangelove retaliation from both Russia and China, followed by a slightly more jittery but no less deadly response from the US, not wanting to be left out during an election year.

I thought about travelling to June 2016. A week before the Brexit vote, to meddle with the results and maybe stick around to influence the US presidential race at the same time. But, when I read up on the newly written history, too much of it was now unfamiliar to me. It wasn't clear how a single, rational man could swing the referendum in the direction of a peace-keeping, border-ignoring Remain. Or indeed, to tweak the US election towards a less paranoid, Democratic future.

So I went back further, much further. A mislaid procurement document during the chaotic events at the Fall of Berlin. This weakened the Russians and strengthened the ties between England and France, with a useful side-effect that the US would never stop being great.

The world ended on the 16th of July 1945. A stack of faded newspapers, the headlines getting larger and larger before the news abruptly stopped, told me how the Trinity Test in New Mexico had far exceeded the scientists' predictions. The first and only nuclear explosion had blown a neat circular hole in the Earth's thin mantle. That might not have been so bad, but a seismic ripple along the length of the Rocky Mountains had unzipped the Yellowstone super-volcano, releasing a million years' worth of magma, all in one short, apocalyptic day. I thought of Oppenheimer's "Now I am become Death, the destroyer of worlds," and, alone and bereft, I wept.

I did not pause to wonder how it was that my bunker was still there, built in 2022 and dependent on post-Singularity technology. Technology that would now never be invented. Kundrat's Conjecture said that it would be impossible to return to a future from which I could not have travelled and, in my serially traumatised state, this I latched onto and blindly accepted.

Scratching my thinning hair, I spotted an opportunity a century earlier. Perhaps I was becoming gung-ho, but it seemed the unsinking of the Titanic was the simplest solution to my – to our – problem.

The world ended because World War I didn't, rumbling on for three arduous decades of chemical and biological warfare. The very lands that were being fought over rendered permanently infertile, the toxins ignoring the contested borders and spreading throughout the whole continent, and beyond.

And so it went on.

The world ended in the fourteenth century, when the Black Death achieved a 95% mortality rate.

The world ended when the Holy Roman Empire became fascinated by quick-silver aphrodisiacs.

The world ended when mankind's Out-of-Africa population bottleneck – the same one that meant our genetic diversity wasn't enough to cope with either the Black Death or the Singularity Virus – led not to vigorous regrowth but instead to slow extinction. The Neanderthals got an extra millennium or so, but still faded away and this time nobody replaced them.

The world ended before it had even begun, the dinosaur-killing asteroid merely grazing the atmosphere. The dinosaurs themselves died out in the climatic changes that followed the breakup of the Pangaean super-continent, but mammals never even got a look-in.

I went back further still, to the very limits of my device, armed this time with a large sledgehammer. Somewhen in the late Proterozoic, I slowly, methodically, and absolutely irreversibly, smashed my time machine, piece by fragile piece, into a million shattered fragments.

The world …

… ENDED

THANK YOU SO much for reading this collection of short stories from the 2020 and 2021 QuaranCon short fiction contests! If you've enjoyed what you've read we'd love it if you would be so kind as to leave a review. Reviews help new readers find our authors!

Also, we encourage you to check out more by these talented authors. You can find them here:

A.M. Justice : www.amjusticeauthor.com

Alex McGilvery : www.alexmcgilvery.com

J E Hannaford : www.jehannaford.com

Laura Shank : www.LauraRshank.com

Anela Deen :www.amidtheimaginary.com

Liam Hogan : www.happyendingnotguaranteed.com

PS Livingstone : www.pslivingstone.com

And to learn more about QuaranCon be sure to check us out at

www.QuaranCon2021.com